Rabbids Invasion

CRACKING UP WITH THE RABBIDS

By David Lewman
Illustrated by Tino Santanach

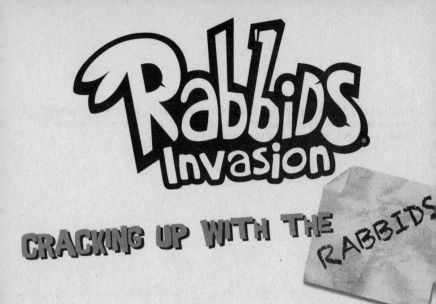

A RABBIDS JOKE BOOK

Simon Spotlight

New York London Toronto Sydney New Delhi

P9-DBY-367

SIMON SPOTLIGHT
An imprint of Simon & Schuster Children's Publishing Division
1230 Avenue of the Americas, New York, New York 10020
This Simon Spotlight edition February 2015
© 2015 Ubisoft Entertainment. All rights reserved. Rabbids, Ubisoft, and the Ubisoft logo are trademarks of Ubisoft Entertainment in the U.S. and/or other countries.
All rights reserved, including the right of reproduction in whole or in part in any form.
SIMON SPOTLIGHT and colophon are registered trademarks of Simon & Schuster, Inc.
For information about special discounts for bulk purchases, please contact Simon & Schuster Special Sales at 1-866-506-1949 or business@simonandschuster.com.
Designed by Jay Colvin
Manufactured in the United States of America 0715 OFF
10 9 8 7 6 5 4 3 2
ISBN 978-1-4814-2790-6
ISBN 978-1-4814-2791-3 (eBook)

The Rabbids are invading planet Earth!

Sounds scary, right?

Wrong!

Everywhere they go, they bring the wacky along with them. While the Rabbids are busy exploring, you'll be busy too—busy laughing.

Follow them as they visit twelve of their favorite hangouts, like the gas station, the drive-through, and the research lab. What would Rabbids do at the gas station? You're about to find out! (Hint: It's going to be funny.)

Get ready, get set, bwah-ha-ha!

RABBIDS AT THE GAS STATION

What's the worst kind of oil to put in your car?
Gargoyle!

How did the gas feel about going in the truck?

Pumped!

When do gas station attendants feel sad?

When they're down in the pumps.

Why was the old tire kicked out of choir?

He was always flat!

What's the best thing to wear when you're hauling a broken car?

A tow-ga!

When is a gas station like a kid eating beans?

When it lets out a lot of gas!

RABBIDS AT THE SUPERMARKET

What did the judge say when the Rabbid snuck into his groceries?

"Order in the cart!"

Which aisle should you never set foot in?

The crocodile!

Why did the grocer kick the Rabbid off the produce scale?

He was in the weigh!

Why did the Rabbid try to pull coins out of the checkout lady's head?

He heard she was the cash-ear!

Where do you buy sludge, muck, and other yucky stuff?

At the gross-ery store!

Who grows the best lunch meat?

The farmer in the deli!

Why did the skunk return to the supermarket?

She forgot to spray for her groceries!

RABBIDS ON THE TENNIS COURT

Why do kings and queens play so much tennis?

They're always in court!

Why did the little old lady hate tennis?

It made such a racket.

Why do tennis pros have so many TVs?

They're always winning sets!

Which tennis player is the best at lighting a campfire?

The player who won the match!

Why did the racquet hit the bad tennis ball?

It served him right!

What's twice as fun as tennis?

Twenty-is!

What do tennis balls say when they're ready to leave?

"Let's bounce!"

RABBIDS AT THE AIRPORT

Why wasn't the fisherman allowed on the plane?

He forgot his boarding bass!

Where do pirates catch planes?

At the *arrr*-port!

Why did the Rabbid strap luggage to his jeans?

He wanted to wear baggy pants!

What's it called when a jet hits you in the throat?

A real plane in the neck!

Why did the pilot cover his plane's wings in sandpaper?

He'd always wanted to work in a skyscraper.

RABBIDS AT THE PARK

What song should you play at a playground wedding?

"Here Comes the Slide."

Which piece of playground equipment attracts the most werewolves?

The hairy-go-round!

What's the most dangerous part of a playground in the jungle?

The quicksand box.

Why did the zombie go to the park?

To get some flesh air.

Which part of the park do predators like the best?

The prey ground.

After he went to two parks in one day. what was the driver ticketed for?

Double-parking.

RABBIDS AT THE FAST-FOOD DRIVE-THROUGH

What did the guy with a cold get at the drive-through?

A double sneeze-booger.

Where do bees get their fast food?

At the hive-through restaurant.

What did the employee say to the skunk?

"May I take your odor?"

What did the employee say to the frog?

"Would you like flies with that?"

Why did the guy think they'd hand him money at the fast-food joint?

He'd heard about their "drive through, win dough."

What did the octopus order at the fast-food joint?

A burger, fries, and a large ink.

RABBIDS AT THE POLAR RESEARCH CENTER

Why did the hula dancer cancel her performance at the North Pole?

She got cold feet.

Why did the traffic cone move to the North Pole?

It wanted to be a snow cone!

Kid 1: Knock, knock.

Kid 2: Who's there?

Kid 1: Icy.

Kid 2: Icy who?

Kid 1: I see it's freezing out here. Let's go back inside!

RABBIDS AT THE ART MUSEUM

Why did the art museum hire a pumpkin?

To be a security gourd.

What did the Rabbids do to the famous painting?

They turned it into a master-in-pieces.

Why did the artist sketch the angry mob?

He wanted to draw a crowd!

Where can you see pictures painted with antlers?

In the moose-eum.

Where can you see pictures painted by ghosts?

In an art ghoul-ery.

RABBIDS AT THE RESEARCH LAB

When is a food research center like a dog?

When it's a chocolate lab.

Why did the scientist leave the lab?

He had to go to the test room.

Why did the Rabbid drape a ram over his shoulders?

He thought he was supposed to wear a lab goat.

What was the vampire scientist most proud of?

His Big Fang Theory.

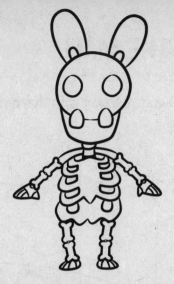

What was the dead scientist most proud of?

His theory of skele-tivity.

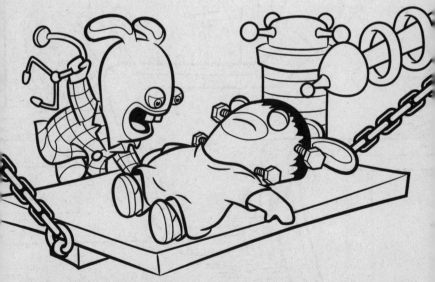

Why did the researcher decide to wear a checked lab coat?

He wanted to be a plaid scientist!

RABBIDS AT THE MALL

What do you call a moving stairway with sharp steps?

An ow-scalator!

What's big and scary and full of merchandise?

A dino-store.

What's the best thing to ride when you go shopping at the mall?

A buy-cycle!

What's the difference between the place in the mall with lots of restaurants and a table with a blanket over it?

One's a food court and the other's a crude fort!

How did the bull pay for the red cloth?

He charged it!

Where can you pass gas and take a photo at the same time?

In the fart-o booth!

RABBIDS IN THE DESERT

Why did the janitor move to the desert?

He wanted to be a dry cleaner.

How did the guy left alone on a sand dune feel?

Deserted.

Why did the guy move to the desert?

He wanted to be the man in the dune.

Knock, knock.

Who's there?

Scott.

Scott who?

'S got to be 120 degrees out here, right?

What's the grouchiest plant in the West?

Grumble-weed.

RABBIDS ON A PIER BY THE OCEAN

Why did the Rabbid punch the pier?

He wanted to hit the deck!

When is a baby like a wooden walkway over the ocean?

When it's a pee-er!

Why is the pier a good place to get sick?
Because there's always a dock around!

What's every Rabbid's favorite song to hear on the pier?
"My Bwah-nnie Lies Over the Ocean!"

Now you've seen all of the Rabbids' favorite haunts—so far, that is—it's time to say bwah-bye! Who knows where they'll explore next? The movie theater? Mount Rushmore? Your backyard?

Wherever it is, the Rabbids will make it . . . bwah-ha-hilarious!